Dear Parents,

Welcome to the Scholastic Reader series. We have taken over 80 years of experience with teachers, parents, and children and put it into a program that is designed to match your child's interests and skills.

Level 1—Short sentences and stories made up of words kids can sound out using their phonics skills and words that are important to remember.

Level 2—Longer sentences and stories with words kids need to know and new "big" words that they will want to know.

Level 3—From sentences to paragraphs to longer stories, these books have large "chunks" of texts and are made up of a rich vocabulary.

Level 4—First chapter books with more words and fewer pictures.

It is important that children learn to read well enough to succeed in school and beyond. Here are ideas for reading this book with your child:

- Look at the book together. Encourage your child to read the title and make a prediction about the story.
- Read the book together. Encourage your child to sound out words when appropriate. When your child struggles, you can help by providing the word.
- Encourage your child to retell the story. This is a great way to check for comprehension.
- Have your child take the fluency test on the last page to check progress.

Scholastic Readers are designed to support your child's efforts to learn how to read at every age and every stage. Enjoy helping your child learn to read and love to read.

> **—Francie Alexander**
> Chief Education Officer
> Scholastic Education

Ms. Frizzle   Liz

Written by Joanna Cole.

Based on *The Magic School Bus* books written by Joanna Cole
and illustrated by Bruce Degen.

The author and editor would like to thank Jonathan D. W. Kahl,
Professor of Atmospheric Sciences at the University of Wisconsin,
for his expert advice in preparing this manuscript.

Illustrations by Carolyn Bracken.

ISBN 0-439-56990-7

12 11   6/0 7/0 8/0 9/0

Designed by Louise Bova & Amy Heinrich

Printed in the U.S.A.
First printing, January 2004

The Magic School Bus®

LOST IN THE SNOW

Arnold   Ralphie   Keesha   Phoebe   Carlos   Tim   Wanda   Dorothy Ann

Cartwheel
·B·O·O·K·S·®

SCHOLASTIC INC.

New York   Toronto   London   Auckland   Sydney
Mexico City   New Delhi   Hong Kong   Buenos Aires

It's fun to be in
Ms. Frizzle's class.

Today we are learning about ice and snow.

ICE AND SNOW
ARE WATER!
by KEESHA
Ice and snow look
different from the
water we drink.
That's because they
are frozen.
   Water freezes
at 32°F (0°C).

WHEN IS SNOW ROUND?

WHEN IT'S A SNOWBALL!

Tim wants to look at snowflakes.
He wants to see them up close.
But no flakes are falling.

Ms. Frizzle drives north.
It gets colder and colder.

The crystals stick
to other crystals.
They make snowflakes.
They start to fall.

When our snowflakes land,
we get big again.
The Friz takes skis out of her bag.
"Put on your skis," she says.

FOLLOW ME, KIDS!

We look in her bag.
There are no skis!
Instead, there are only
ice skates.

MS. FRIZZLE MADE A MISTAKE!

THAT'S NOT LIKE MS. FRIZZLE.

We see a ski house.
It is far away.
Maybe Ms. Frizzle is
waiting for us there.

NEVER, EVER
SKATE UNLESS
AN ADULT
SAYS IT'S OK

SAFE
TO SKATE
This ice is
OKAY.
A ranger
tested it.

We come to a frozen lake.
The ski house is on the other side.
We skate across the lake.

Poof! Now our skates are gone.
We head toward the ski house,
but the snow is deep.
It's so deep we cannot walk.

Then we hear something.

Surprise!
It's Ms. Frizzle and
the Magic School Bus!
But the bus is *not* a bus.

Fluency Fun:

The words in each list below end in the same sounds.
Read the words in a list.
Read them again.
Read them faster.
Try to read all 15 words in one minute.

found	falling	funny
pound	going	fuzzy
round	learning	icy
ground	looking	snowy
around	waiting	tiny

Look for these words in the story.

different   **water**   **gone**

instead   **toward**

Note to Parents:
According to *A Dictionary of Reading and Related Terms,* fluency is "the ability to read smoothly, easily, and readily with freedom from word-recognition problems." Fluency is necessary for good comprehension and enjoyable reading. The activities on this page include a speed drill and a sight-recognition drill. Speed drills build fluency because they help students rapidly recognize common syllables and spelling patterns in words, and they're fun! Sight-recognition drills help students smoothly and accurately recognize words. Practice these activities with your child to help him or her become a fluent reader.
                                    –Wiley Blevins,
                                    Reading Specialist